Pudges
House

by Hiawyn
Oram
+
Tim Warnes

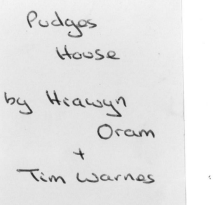

For William Robert
H.O.

For Michelle and our cardboard boxes
T.W.

PUFFIN BOOKS

Published by the Penguin Group
Penguin Books Ltd, 80 Strand, London WC2R 0RL, England
Penguin Group (USA), Inc., 375 Hudson Street, New York, New York 10014, USA
Penguin Books Australia Ltd, 250 Camberwell Road, Camberwell, Victoria 3124, Australia
Penguin Books Canada Ltd, 10 Alcorn Avenue, Toronto, Ontario, Canada M4V 3B2
Penguin Books India (P) Ltd, 11 Community Centre, Panchsheel Park, New Delhi – 110 017, India
Penguin Books (NZ) Ltd, Cnr Rosedale and Airborne Roads, Albany, Auckland, New Zealand
Penguin Books (South Africa) (Pty) Ltd, 24 Sturdee Avenue, Rosebank 2196, South Africa

Penguin Books Ltd, Registered Offices: 80 Strand, London WC2R 0RL, England

www.penguin.com

First published in 2004
1 3 5 7 9 10 8 6 4 2

Set in Monotype Bembo Schoolbook

Manufactured in China

British Library Cataloguing in Publication Data
A CIP catalogue record for this book is available from the British Library

ISBN Hardback 0–670–91135–6
ISBN Paperback 0–140–56857–3

PUDGE'S HOUSE

Hiawyn Oram ★ Tim Warnes

PUFFIN BOOKS

Pudge's mum and dad had bought a new television.

They were very pleased with it …

and Pudge and his friend Gus were
very pleased with its box.

"It's my new house," said Pudge, climbing in.

"Just the kind of very own new house I've
always been looking for."

Pudge and Gus played in Pudge's
new house all morning.

They had lunch in it.

They took their afternoon nap in it.

They wiggled it around so they could watch the new television from the window they'd made in it.

Then Gus's mum came to take him home and Pudge had to go to the bathroom.

When he came back his house
was not where he'd left it.

"It's outside," said his dad. "Your mum doesn't want a big box all over the living room."

"But it's not a box!" wailed Pudge.
"It's my house! My very own new house that
I've always been looking for!"

He ran outside to the dustbins.

Pudge dragged his house to the upstairs landing and jumped right in.

"Now I can watch my house when I
have to go to the bathroom," he announced,
"because that's the only time I'm coming out, EVER!"

Just then, the doorbell rang.

It was Pudge's friends, Kid, Peebs and Kitty.

"We were just on our way to the park,"

said Kid's mum, "to try out the new swings.

Would Pudge like to come?"

"I don't think so," said Pudge's mum. "You see, he's upstairs in his new house and he's never coming out, except to go to the bathroom, EVER."

"Then we'd better go up and see him," said Kid.
So Kid and Peebs and Kitty went upstairs to see Pudge.

"Hello," said Pudge through his window.

"Isn't this a great house?"

"It is," said Peebs.

"Though it could also just be a box,"
said Kitty, "with a hole in it."

"When you want to go to the park," said Kid.

"And that's just what it will be!" cried Pudge,
jumping out and running downstairs.

"But, Pudge," cried his mum, "what about your house that you're never coming out of?"
"Oh, that," Pudge called back.
"Right now it's just a big box with a big hole in it! But don't throw it away …"

"Because," he said to his friends, as they swung on the new swings and slid on the slide, "when we get back it'll be my new house again!"

"And my new house!" said Kitty.

"And my new house!" said Peebs.

"And my new house!" said Kid.

"Just the kind of house we've always been looking for!" they all said together. And it was!